PROTECTING ELENA

DENNIS'S DARKNESS

BY

MIKE CAGE

Summary

Dennis, who works for the CIA, has just completed their latest mission and goes to the bar in Las Vegas, as is his ritual after every successful mission. There, he manages to save a busty blonde who offers him a bit of kinky fun.

Dennis rejects this offer because the terrible memories of his past have been triggered. (He's a foster with a sordid past.)

The next day, his best friend, Adam, invites him to drink with his sister. Dennis gives in after slight coercion and gets to meet Adam's sister, Elena, whom he considers young but absolutely gorgeous. Adam leaves the bar with a woman, and Elena ends up in Dennis's apartment, where their first kiss happens. Adam, the next morning, finds out that his cover has been blown and so he has to keep Elena safe, as she could possibly become a target.

<u>Copyright</u> © _[MIKE CAGE]

What The Story Covers

- Dennis visits a bar where he saves a busty blonde from a drunk bloke who tries to assault her.
- He's awoken from a nightmare by his best friend's phone call for drinks.
- Dennis meets Elena, his best friend's sister, whom he considers a little too young, a hasty assumption that he later finds out he's totally wrong about.
- Adam's heartache leads him to making some pretty bad decisions, like leaving the bar with a woman who blows his cover.
- Dennis and Elena become panicky as they search the whole bar for Adam.
- Dennis finds Elena insanely attractive but is afraid she's too young due to her slender body and youthful look.
- They end up leaving the bar and going to Dennis's home, where their first kiss happens.
- Tension rises as Elena makes a show of proving that she is not a late teen by mildly seducing Dennis into a heated kiss that they both feel down to their toes.
- Their moment is interrupted by Barton, Dennis's superior, who announces Adam's blown cover and the danger that could possibly lie ahead.
- Elena, who could become a primary target, is to be kept safe as Adam has been brought back to the facility.
- Elena stubbornly refuses to go to a safe facility upon Dennis's suggestion.
- Dennis has to take her to his home in Arizona, a long drive from Vegas. But they make a stop at a hotel to spend the night on their way, and there, they are faced with some pretty bad men who are already tailing them.
- Dennis pulls a ridiculous stunt to keep their identities hidden; kisses Elena again.

Table of Contents

Chapter One

People were born with different gifts, talents, and attributes that made them stand out. For Dennis Carnell, he seemed to have a little bit of everything, from his ability to tell when he was in the wrong crowd to sniffing out assailants and rogues.

It had to have taken years of practice to be this good. During his training, his superiors had even told him that he was a natural. His abilities extended to other people, including...women. Dennis could tell a woman wanted him in the same way he knew the blonde leaning against the wall on the far side of the bar he was currently in did.

He had come here straight from his last mission, a terribly fantastic habit he had formed during his early years in the field. He'd usually leave with a woman who caught his fancy, but not tonight. Tonight, there was something else entirely on his mind.

Even though the blonde lady was doing a very good job of pretending she wasn't watching him, Dennis could tell when her gaze would flicker his direction. He also did not need to turn in her direction to know that she was.

Dennis continued to nurse his drink, his eyes scanning the growing crowd of dancers from time to time. It wasn't abnormal for a fight in this sort of scene to break out, or for a woman who was trying to have a good time to be assaulted. Dennis had, quite a number of times, punched quite a number of jaws. Most men tended to think with their nether regions when uninhibited—

"Leave me the hell alone," someone shouted from the far side of the bar.

Dennis, who had learned to pick out peculiar noises even in booming rooms, tensed up, already aware of what was about to happen.

"I said to leave me alone!" The voice shouted again, the tone cracking at the end of it to signal their obvious fear, which was why Dennis was suddenly turning towards the direction the ruckus was coming from, his glass of whiskey abandoned.

Fist already balled, Dennis moved towards the corner of the bar, which was slightly shrouded in darkness. There, the blonde lady was plastered against the wall, her hands thrust out to keep the stupid bloke who was leaning over her at bay. Her eyes were wild, and her hands slightly shook.

There was a chuckle from the drunk bloke who was inching closer and closer to the scared blonde, until his chest met the woman's quivering hands. Dennis could tell that he was relishing the fear he could read in her eyes. It looked like he was getting off on her vulnerability, and the sight almost had Dennis slamming the stupid drunk against the far side of the wall. But he held off on doing that.

"Pretty gals don't say that, dear," the drunk sneered, loud enough for Dennis to hear. "Now, be a good girl and drop those shaking hands before I break them."

"Not if I break yours first," Dennis said, stepping close enough for them to take him in. Even though the man was a head taller than the blonde, Dennis towered over them both, his prominent muscle weight causing the wide-eyed man to gulp.

"What do you want?" the man asked. "This is none of your business; she's my girlfriend."

The blonde girl maniacally shook her head no. But Dennis paid her no mind, already pissed off by the stupid man who was clearly expecting him to do as he said. Dennis took a closer look at him, taking in the suits he wore, slightly creased in notable places. He was clearly the office type who got to give orders and boss fellow employees around.

Dennis didn't need to step closer to the duo for his voice to carry through to them. "If you don't step away from her right this second, I'm going to do more than just break your fingers."

Now, there was real fear in the man's eyes as he met Dennis's eyes. He reluctantly stepped away from the blonde, who already had a relieved look on her face, but didn't get completely out of sight like he expected him to. Instead, he stepped closer to him and said. "You know that girls like this love it when you play with them. Don't act like a saint, like you wouldn't do the exact same thing—"

Dennis did it before thinking, allowing his fist to connect with the man's jaw. There was a definite crack and a scream. "What the fuck, man?" the man asked, but Dennis, who was already seeing red, held him by the collar of his shirt and smashed him hard against the wall, shaking him so hard his teeth chattered and his eyes rolled to the back of his head.

"I'm s-sorry. Please, o-oh God, I'm going to die. I'm sorry man, I didn't mean that."

Dennis could feel hands trying to pry him away from the man. A second later, he moved his hands away, not waiting to see the wheezing man drop to the floor like a bag of unpeeled potatoes. He was already on his way out, his hands still shaking from rage.

A small crowd had gathered to watch the scene, and Dennis hated that he had brought attention to himself in that manner. As he made his way to the door, he felt suffocated, like he couldn't breathe. The man's words had poked at a memory he thought he had buried for good.

He rarely ever lost his cool like that. And his hands very rarely shook from the sort of rage they were doing now. Dennis moved purposefully to his car, the need to escape from the bar and the feelings that were currently coursing through him almost making him howl.

The moment he pulled his car door open, a voice sounded behind him. "Hey, wait." Dennis tensed up once again and slowly turned around. It was the blonde lady. She was panting slightly when she got close enough for him to hear.

Dennis slammed his car door shut and leaned against it. The woman came to stand in front of him, whatever feminine perfume she had worn drifting to his nostrils. "You saved me back there."

Dennis chuckled. "I'm no savior." Taking a closer look at her, Dennis realized she could not have been older than twenty, even though her chest looked a bit unnaturally generous and her waist thin.

"No, you really did." She laughed, but without humor." The man was pretty much convinced I was a call girl and was literally trying to force me to—"

Dennis lifted a hand to stall her, not sure he wanted the details of what the man had tried to coerce her to do. "You don't have to tell me."

The woman blinked at him and nodded. "No, I don't. Thank you."

Dennis nodded and stepped away to pull his car's door open once again. "You should go home though," he advised. "I think you've had enough fun for one night."

"I should," she said, biting her lower lips that looked a bit too wide for her small face. "I didn't come with a car." Dennis found himself shutting his door again at her words. He studied her a little closely; her eyes seemed a little glazed. How many glasses had the damn woman had?

"I could call you a taxi," he suggested

"Or you could take me home instead." She looked bolder, her shoulders squared in determination. Was it just him or had she suddenly thrust out her chest more?

"I am not looking for company tonight," Dennis said.

The woman had the decency to blush, her head ducked coyly. "I didn't mean it like that. I meant to just drop me off."

Dennis nodded. "I think I can manage that." The woman breathed out and followed him to the passenger side, where he held the door open for her to get in.

Dennis shut the door behind her and strode quickly to the driver's side. "I'm going to need your home address, ma'am."

"My name is Zoe," she said with a wince. "Ma'am makes me feel like my grandmother."

"Dennis," he offered curtly.

After Zoe had given him her home address, Dennis punched it into the navigation system and expertly maneuvered the car out of the parking lot. The silence in the car was not comfortable, but Dennis had no intention of breaking it. He was still lost in thought at the memories that had surged to the surface. Memories he thought he'd had a tight lid on.

"Are you a cop?" Dennis hears Zoe blurt out.

Dennis turned to the woman, giving her an amused smile. "What gave it away?"

Zoe rolled her eyes. "I think you're a cop. You'd managed to know something was wrong in a darkened crowd full of screaming bodies. I'd really thought that this man was going to have his way..." Her voice trailed away as if she was reliving that moment, and then she added, her voice a little quieter. "I really do wonder how you'd know."

Dennis shrugged. "My sixth sense must be spot on, I guess." Even though that was half the truth, Dennis was not willing to reveal more.

"It's really sort of funny how someone I'd clearly not wanted came onto me, when the one I'd actually been fixated on the whole time didn't."

Dennis tensed up at her words but tried to feign ignorance at it, even though he knew she had pretty much been focused on him the entire night. "There was someone you fancied?" he asked.

"You." She answered, turning to him. "And now, I have an added reason to be grateful you were there. I want to pay you back." She stated it simply.

"What?" This time, his ignorance was not faked.

"I want to show you my gratitude," she explained, painted fingernails moving sensually up his thigh to the hole in his distressed jeans. Her fingers were warm, but it ignited a cold inside of him that caused him to nearly run the car off the road.

"Stop." It was out of his mouth before he knew it.

"What?" The woman asked, confused. "You don't want this?"

"I am not looking for company tonight." He explained, plucking her hands off his skin.

The woman seemed to balk at his words, as if she could not believe he was being real. "You mean you don't want to have sex?"

"That's another way of putting it," he said, hoping to let her down as mildly as possible. There was no need to make this more awkward than it already was.

"Men always want sex," was what the blonde said as she sat back in a state of disbelief.

"I'm no saint, believe me," he joked as he glided into a suburban area. "You live alone?" he asked.

Zoe turned to him with a smirk. "Why? Will you come in for some tea?" She made tea sound nothing like bringing a cup of brown liquid to the lips.

Dennis chuckled and slid into a driveway that faced a townhouse. And then, he turned to her and said, "If you didn't look like you'd just graduated from high school five months ago, I'd have your leg wrapped around my waist and then have you put that sharp tongue of yours to good use."

Zoe, who was probably shocked at his words, blinked several times, her jaw unhinged. Chuckling once more to himself, Dennis slid out of the car and went to her side to open it. When she finally got a hold of herself and stepped out, she staggered a little.

Had she been drunk all along? Good thing he'd had no intention of bedding her. "I wish you'd do more than you could talk," she whispered as she shuffled past him, ensuring that her ample chest brushed against his. She looked into his eyes, hers darkened from whatever makeup she'd put on. Her lips moved slowly to his jaw, where she mouthed against the stubbled chin. "I am also very older than eighteen," she whispered against the skin of his sculpted jaw. "In case you were wondering."

The feel of those breasts against his front was awesome, but a warm willing body was not going to cut it for him; he was going to need more than that. Dennis stepped back and gave her a smile. "Have a great night, Zoe," he said and turned away from her, moving back to the driver's side.

This time, when he glanced at her, there was a smile playing on those generous lips. She lifted a hand in greeting and stepped away from the car towards the door. Even though it wasn't the first time he had turned a woman down, Dennis had a feeling that a light friendship with Zoe was one he would have immensely enjoyed. Pity that he hadn't gotten her number.

Chapter Two

Dennis spent a better part of the night tossing and turning, plagued with memories he no longer had a lid on. When he finally did doze off, it happened again.

"You whore. Why'd you come back by this time?" the man yelled.

"I had to work extra time. Meredith, my colleague—"

"Was right in that store because I went there myself," the man roared. "Now, find another lie." In a deadly voice, he said, stepping closer to the shivering woman, "Wanna be a little slut? You want to give your body to those men for free, huh? You stupid piece of—"

Dennis snapped awake with a gasp, skin glistening with sweat, light pants puffing from parted lips. After nearly two decades, the memories still plagued him, his past unwilling to let him out of its vice-like grip. It didn't matter how many exterminators he apprehended or the big guns he saved, because at night, he was a little kid again, cowering in a corner, helpless. Just like his sister was.

The phone line ringing was jarring enough to cause Dennis's heart to skip a beat. When he realized it was the landline, Dennis got out of bed and moved to the living room.

"Dennis Carnell's residence," he barked.

"Denny."

Dennis shut his eyes and breathed in deeply. "Adam." He said, his tone quiet.

Adam chuckled. "What are you doing? Wrapped around some woman?"

"I would not be on the phone if I were." Dennis chuckled, his anxiety already dissipating a little. Adam was his partner, but Dennis saw him as more than that. They'd gone on so many missions together, constantly having each other's backs. Adam was no longer a colleague; he was a brother.

"Good thing the boss gave us a week off. I know that you, my friend, are going to make the most of it," Adam teased.

"That might not happen if you intend to keep me on the phone."

Adam chuckled. "I just might have been brought into your life to ruin your plans."

Dennis shook his head at his friend. "What do you want, Adam?"

"For you to come back out? Join us in the land of the living?" Adam said it like it was a suggestion, but Dennis knew he was going to hound him until he gave in. Barton had given them a week off pending an assignment overseas. They were both professionals who understood why they needed to lay low until the assignment was completed. But Adam, whose mantra was living life on the edge, would say he was not cut out for that nonsense.

"My little sister came to town. Remember Elena?" Adam asked, his voice slurring a little. "She's going to be at my place in an hour, and I'd love for us to show her around. She's never been to Las Vegas. And I did promise her that if I was ever to get assigned here, I'd invite her over."

Dennis frowned. "Isn't that dangerous, dude? Your cover could be blown."

"My cover is not gonna be blown. Come on, Denny. Live a little."

Dennis bared his teeth in a silent growl. "You know, I hate it when you call me that. And there's no way I am strutting Las Vegas with you when we just completed an assignment that has some pretty bad boys up our asses."

Adam made a pfft sound. "As if they've ever sniffed us out." Which was sort of true. Both Adam and Dennis worked for the CIA and had never failed an assignment. There had been times they'd pretty much felt invincible, but it didn't mean that Dennis was still unaware of the repercussions of having their cover blown. The scientist whose research work they'd destroyed had worked hand-in-hand with the Russian government, and even though Dennis and Adam refused to admit it to themselves, it had been the most dangerous assignment they'd worked on.

"It's not going to be just me. My younger sister would be there. She'd be so excited," Adam said in a bid to convince him.

"Isn't she still a little kid?"

Dennis could practically hear Adam's eyes roll. "Elena is an adult who's grown enough to have drinks."

Dennis shook his head at his friend, prepared to say no, but Adam, who knew him too well, said, "You wouldn't want my sister and me to weave around the streets of Fermont Street unguarded, would you? We both know I have always been the nerd. I do not have the sort of muscles you do to ward off—"

"Okay, okay," Dennis conceded, not quite believing that he was agreeing to this. "But we will stick to the books, okay? You're here as a tourist. We absolutely cannot blow our cover."

Adam's response was a chuckle. "Cut me some slack, dude. There's no way that's going to happen. We've done this long enough for me to waste away the rest of this week with my eyes closed without giving anything away."

Adam was one of the best they had. Dennis believed him when he said he wouldn't do anything to blow their cover. "Good," Dennis said, as they made arrangements for them to meet up at Dennis's temporary residence right there in Vegas.

Dennis couldn't go back to bed and was glad for the distracting phone call that had taken his mind off his thoughts. But as he moved to the fully stocked kitchen to make himself a cup of coffee, his mind went back to the nightmare of last night. He shook his head and valiantly pushed the memory to the back burner. Today wasn't going to be one of those days.

Three hours later, the doorbell sounded as Dennis stepped out of the shower. He swiftly slipped on his pants and, without bothering with a shirt, moved to the door to let Adam in. Even though he vaguely remembered being shown a picture of Adam's kid sister, he wasn't ready to find a beautiful brunette on his doorstep with translucent blue eyes and lips that looked like they were begging to be kissed.

"Hey man," Adam greeted him as Dennis stepped back to let them in.

"Hey," Dennis said, forcing his eyes away from the enchanting sight of the woman who was staring at him, her eyes roving over his bare torso.

Dennis led Adam and his sister to the living room, amused when he met the girl's eyes again and noticed her cheeks reddening. How old had Adam said she was again?

Adam made introductions, and Dennis politely took Elena's hand in a handshake, nearly gasping when shocks rose up his forearm. If Elena had felt it too, he couldn't tell, but her cheeks did seem to become even redder.

Adam smelled faintly of alcohol, and Dennis, for the life of him, could not understand how one could drink so early. Dennis remembered his words slurring a little as they'd spoken on the phone earlier. He shook his head at his friend and moved back quickly to the room to pull on a shirt. When he was back out, Elena looked like she was more herself. Her cheeks were no longer red, and her eyes were on her phone screen, a light smile playing on those heart-shaped lips.

Dennis surreptitiously studied her, noting the skinny jeans and shirt. She looked laid-back and not at all like someone who would draw attention to herself, thereby getting them both in trouble, which was exactly something they needed to avoid.

Dennis found that it was a bit awkward trying to communicate with Adam in Elena's presence. What could they even talk about with her present? Dennis had never discussed his family with Adam. Although Adam must have been aware that he was a foster kid. After all, the facility had his files. But he'd never directly asked; no one had. Well, except, of course, Barton, the only man who seemed to not be swerved by who Dennis became when asked personal questions like that.

And Dennis had needed to answer Barton's probing questions during cross-examination. It was the only way he could have been kept in the field. Barton was the only one who came close to getting all the sordid details about his past. Even then, Dennis had still managed to put up walls. Reliving his past in such a gruesome manner was something he wasn't going to let happen.

Dennis turned to Adam and gave him the look, and gave a subtle glance in Elena's direction. Adam stared at him a bit confusedly, his eyes narrowed. A second later, he understood the silent question and said. "Oh. Yes, she knows."

Dennis balked. "She does?"

"Yes. She's family and it's not like she will go shout it on a rooftop at the top of her lungs."

"What are you both talking about?" Elena asked, her light blue eyes switching to Dennis, who felt like a deer caught in the headlights. He had never floundered in a woman's presence and wondered what it was about the young woman that threw him off in this manner.

Adam chuckled and turned to his little sister. "Denny wanted to know if you know that I do, in fact, work for the government."

"None of his family knows?" Elena asked in blatant confusion. And even though Dennis knew that the question wasn't asked with any malicious intent, it didn't stop it from hitting him like a suckerpunch. Adam, who must have noticed his reaction, shifted uneasily in his seat.

"I wouldn't know. It's a personal choice we all make." Adam explained to a still confused-looking Elena, who switched those eyes back to him. "I'm sorry," she said, making it obvious that she was privy to his current discomfort.

Dennis shrugged it off and stood to his feet, suddenly feeling suffocated. "We should head out now," he said, and Adam jumped up to join him, looking immensely relieved. Apparently, he wasn't the only one to notice tension.

"Why don't we get breakfast somewhere first and maybe head out for a few drinks?"

Dennis turned to glare at Adam in the passenger seat beside him. Drinks? Adam had been acting really weird, and he couldn't for the life of him understand why. Did he not realize how dangerous it was for them to take a family member to their place of assignment, as well as how dangerous it was for said family member?

Dennis could not resist taking a closer look at Adam, his eyes widening when he realized what had been happening all along. Adam was in a tailspin!

Dennis looked up at the rearview mirror, his eyes meeting Elena's own. "Is he alright?" he murmured, unable to help himself. Adam had tilted his head to the side and was looking out the window with a forlorn look on his face.

Elena's eyes darkened with sadness as she shook her head no. Dennis turned to study Adam out of the corner of his eyes while still managing to keep his gaze on the road. Now, he could make out the dark circles beneath his eyes and how sad they were. Adam's four-year relationship had ended because, apparently, there was no way Lois, his girlfriend, was going to stomach being with a man who faked identities and traveled several countries in a month.

Adam had seemed to take the loss in a manner that even Dennis had admired. Dennis should have dug deeper because, like him, a lot of them were used to masking pain. Dennis had lived with his own agony and the trauma of his past for years. Not even Adam knew anything about his childhood and his abusive foster parents.

With renewed knowledge, Dennis continued towards the restaurant, determined to help his friend out of his funk in any way he could before his grief landed them both in trouble.

Chapter Three

Dennis drove silently to an understated bar on the outskirts of town. He was no longer interested in showing little Elena around, not when Adam needed obvious help. They were supposed to lay low, and not use placards to announce their presence in Las Vegas.

They all stepped into the bar, and Dennis scanned the sparse crowd, noting a woman who sat in a corner, nursing her drink on her own. The bartender was a middle-aged man with a growing pot belly. He didn't look like the type to spy on clients for seedy men, but Dennis could never be too sure. He had learned from his job to never judge anyone by their appearance.

They moved to a seat in the slightly darkened corner of the bar that afforded them a little bit of privacy. Adam, who had seemed to shake off his earlier mood, grinned at him. "I really want to get shitfaced."

Dennis understood Adam's desire to drink his pain away. The earlier sadness was still evident in his eyes. Now that he knew what was up and what to look for, he could very well see it. "We are not teenagers, Adam." Adults didn't even use phrases like that. Was it even a good idea to be out here?

But Adam was already moving to the bar to order for them. Dennis shook his head at his friend and turned to Elena, who had been silently regarding him. "You care about him, don't you?" she said.

"He's like a brother to me. We practically grew up in the academy together."

Elena, who was still studying him, nodded. "He spoke a lot about you each time he'd return. He still does. You're like his older, supernova brother."

Dennis allowed the compliment to slide away, not quite knowing what to do with it. "What is really going on with him? How long has he been like this?"

Elena looked sadly out the window. "I am not here to see what Las Vegas looks like. I'm here to look after him."

Dennis's eyes widened. He blinked rapidly, trying to understand what Elena meant. "You didn't come here to tour the city?"

"Not with a distraught brother, no." Elena sighed deeply. "I really need that drink to get through this."

"Adam will bring them over," Dennis assured, silently motioning for her to continue. She began, "I don't know if you know about Lois and their recent breakup."

"Yes. They were engaged to be married."

"Lois is tying the knot with another man today."

"Oh." This explains why Adam was spiraling, and why he'd been drinking so early. He was trying to numb the pain.

"I think Adam knows that Lois wasn't exactly faithful during their time together. It was so easy for her to break things off with him and hitch it with the current bloke. So, I think her faithlessness hurts Adam even more than her betrayal."

Dennis scrubbed his hands over his face as memories of his own betrayal cascaded over him—the woman he had loved once, who had also managed to ruin him in the cruelest way possible. It seemed like he was constantly stifling one terrible memory after another.

"It hurts more than words could ever describe," Dennis rasped in agreement. Elena looked at him and he looked back, noting how the sun reflecting off of her eyes made them look so beautifully translucent that it was almost surreal.

Elena was so beautiful, it was a bit distracting. And she was currently looking at him like she wanted him to say more, talk more about his past. Something that was never, ever going to happen.

A second later, there was a loud thud on the table. Adam had returned with their drinks. Dennis promptly picked up his and brought it to his lips, taking a careful sip and sighing gratefully as the powerful tonic slid down his throat.

Adam, who had not sat yet, said to no one in particular, "I happen to see a woman I fancy seated there all by herself. I'm going to go talk to her, alright? See if her mind is as sexy as her body. I love me some sexy women."

Elena simply rolled her eyes and picked up her own drink.

"Are you old enough to drink that?" Dennis blurted it out without thinking. How old was the woman again? Didn't Adam say she was 20?

Elena, who currently looked peeved, asked, "What do you mean by that?"

"How old are you?"

Elena barked out a laugh that sounded humorless and dry, even to his own ears. "I've been assumed to be a lot of things, but never have I been accused of being an underage drinker."

"You can tell me how old you are, and we can both be done with this awkward conversation," Dennis said with a tight frown.

"No, I will not do that, not after you've managed to see me as a woman not older than 23. What is it about my body that would even remotely suggest that to you?"

Dennis looked back at her, perplexed. Was she being serious? Had she never looked at her body in the mirror? With deliberate slowness, Dennis allowed his eyes to scan the woman's body, starting from her rich brown curls to her straight, ridiculously perfect nose.

Dennis took in the tiny mole at the corner of her lips, and suddenly the urge to taste it slammed into him. He blinked and looked away. He could not be attracted to Elena. No, it had to be anyone but her.

But then, his eyes went back to her, silently nursing her drink, and he found his gaze running over her muscle shirt. Elena was willowy, and her curves, if there were any hidden beneath her clothes, were barely obvious.

"Like what you see?" came an amused voice.

Dennis, who knew he had been caught checking her out, just shrugged, hoping he had managed to pull off the look of disinterest. But when his hazel eyes met those gleaming blues, he saw in them passion and genuine interest.

"25," she stated.

"What?" Dennis, who was in a state of confusion, asked.

"I mean that I am 25."

Dennis shook his head. She really was not a teenager, even though she had the body of one. "And I am done with college, so don't ever assume I'm not old enough to drink."

Dennis, feeling properly chastised, nodded. And they both scanned the crowd, looking for Adam, who was suddenly nowhere to be found. Panic seized Dennis's throat and he was up on his feet before he realized it, moving through the growing crowd.

He couldn't believe what had just happened. He had been so caught up in his discussion with Elena that he had not even kept an eye on Adam like he was here to.

"What's going on? Where's my brother?" Elena asked, her voice shaking slightly. Like him, she had probably examined the crowd and seen no sign of him.

"I cannot find him anywhere." He said, worry and fear seizing his throat. He pulled his phone out of his pocket and dialed Adam's number as they moved towards what appeared to be the loo.

"He went to meet some woman who was sitting in the far corner over there," Dennis explained, as they both automatically began to move in that direction. There was no sign of the woman, but there were indeed two glasses on the table. Had Adam left with the woman, or had he somehow been muscled out of there without their knowledge?

But even as Dennis thought about it, he knew that there was no way something like that would have happened. Either Adam had gone home with the woman or he was playing one of his stupid pranks on them. And if it was the latter, there was no way this was funny.

When the call went straight to voicemail, Dennis's heart sank.

"Can't get through to him?" Elena's eyes were filled with worry and fear.

Dennis, who did not want her to worry, shook his head. "But I think he's safe; there's no way he could be dragged out of here without us knowing. He's probably here somewhere." Dennis went on to reassure. "Why don't you check the loo while I scout the whole place?"

Elena nodded and began to jog away, but Dennis pulled her back to himself and said, "Give me your phone."

"Why?" she asked, her eyes narrowed.

Was he the bad man here? Why the hell was she looking at him with such distrust?

"Can you give me the damn phone? I need to be able to reach you."

"But I'm simply going to check—"

"Are you going to give me the damn phone or not?" For all they knew, Adam could be lying in a ditch somewhere. And if it had actually happened, it was not going to be the first time someone from the academy had had their cover blown and then killed. But he hoped very much that this wasn't the case. He couldn't bear the loss of Adam. Not in this lifetime.

He punched in his number into her phone and handed it back. "Call me if anything is up."

Elena nodded without argument, and they both turned away at the same time, Dennis striding to the bartender whom he had noticed look over at them a couple of times. He no longer had a good feeling about what was going on, and his intuition never failed him.

He watched the bartender as he inched closer, noting the way his fingers shook slightly. Dennis dropped onto the seat directly in front of him. "Seen a guy about 5 feet tall around here? With a buzz cut?"

The bartender chuckled as he continued to mix drinks."I've seen a dozen guys with a buzz cut since I resumed my shift."

"Well, I was hoping you'd tell me he had gone home with the woman he was sitting in the far corner with. I have the hots for his sister, but he would kill me if he found us out. I need to know he went home with the woman so I can bring his sister to my place."

This caught the bartender's attention, and he grinned. "Is it the hot brunette you were speaking with earlier?" he asked, baring his crooked teeth in a smile.

Dennis fake-grinned. "Yeah, that one."

"I don't know everyone who leaves with people here, but I'd say I saw someone that fits your description leave with a woman. They appeared to have been flirting their socks off. I'm sure you'd be safe if you banged his kid sis all night."

Dennis tried not to wince at the bartender's crude words. "That's all the reassurance I needed," Dennis grinned, his cheeks already hurting from faking smiles.

The bartender's grin was even wider as he said, "Good luck."

"We are all going to need it," Dennis muttered. He hadn't gleaned anything about the bartender and hoped against hope that the pot-bellied man wasn't a spy. Dennis began to move towards the direction of the restroom, relieved to find Elena picking her way through the long line.

"Have you found him?" she worriedly asked.

Dennis shook his head no. "We have to get out of here. Stay close to me," he advised as they began to move through the sea of bodies, through a back door Dennis had scanned.

Dennis pulled out his phone as soon as they stepped outside into the midmorning air and dialed Adam again, and this time, he did answer.

"Sup man," Adam slurred.

Weak with relief, Dennis asked, "Where the hell are you?"

"Relax," Adam said. "I went home with the cute redhead. I'll be over at your place to pick up my sister, alright? She wants us to do some kinky shit, dude. I'm about to have the best sex of my life. Talk later." Adam disconnected.

Dennis blinked several times and turned back to meet Elena's questioning stare. "Was that him? What did he say?"

Dennis, who was still in a state of shock, said, "Sounds like you're going to have to spend the night at my place."

Chapter Four

The ride was filled with tense silence. "Why can't I stay over at Adam's?" Elena stubbornly asked.

"Because it would be unsafe."

"How unsafe can being in an enclosed space be?"

"Do you know how to use a gun?"

"What?" she asked, her eyes wide.

"Adam has a short pistol. Do you know how to use it? If something happened, would you be able to cock the gun and shoot at an assailant?"

Elena slowly shook her head and said nothing else, which settled it. She was going to have to spend the night at his place, something Dennis didn't want to think too deeply about. His temporary apartment had just one room. There'd been no need to request something bigger from the academy, but at that moment he truly wished he had.

He watched Elena out of the corner of his eyes, unable to help himself. She was looking out the window, her face turned away from him. The closer they got to the apartment, the tenser the car ride got.

When Dennis pulled into the garage, Elena stepped out of the car as if being in an enclosed space with him had been suffocating. Dennis mirrored her movement, and together, they took the elevator to Dennis's wing.

When they stepped into the apartment, Elena looked around, as if seeing it for the first time.

"Would you like something to drink?"

"Sparkling water, please," Elena said.

Dennis moved to his little kitchenette, all the while thinking about how the hell the sleeping arrangement was going to go. There was no way he was going to climb into bed with Elena. He was going to have to take the couch, wasn't he?

Dennis settled on the couch after handing Elena her glass of water and tried not to watch her like a creep.

"I'm sorry for putting you out."

"You're not."

"Are you sure about that? That you don't want me out of your hair?"

Dennis wanted her in his hair, in his bed where they could do things that Adam absolutely did not have to know, but he couldn't tell her that. Dennis had found Elena attractive from the moment he had opened his door to them this morning.

And now, being in a room alone with her was more tempting than anything had the right to be. Maybe this was purely hormonal. It had been so long since he had last bedded a woman that he really should have fucked Zoe when she practically begged for it because now he wouldn't be grappling with self-control with his best friend's sister.

"I don't want you out of my hair because I want you to be safe. And safety means keeping you here with me."

Elena smiled at his words, making him feel like he had said something right. "Adam has always had a thing for redheads."

Dennis shook his head. "There's no way I'm discussing your brother's love life with you."

Elena chuckled. "Why?"

Dennis made a funny face. "It's weird, Elena. First, you're his sister. Second, I don't want to imagine what he gets up to or what he could be currently doing." He had said something about kink. Dennis really hoped his dear friend was playing it safe. "And you're young, too," he added as his gaze traveled over her long, lean body. Were there really curves beneath those clothes? Oh what Dennis would have given to find out... When his face moved back up, he found those beautiful eyes riveted on him, lips slightly parted.

But then, Elena sat up right in front of him, crossed one leg over the other, and fixed him with a hot stare. "You think I'm too young?" Elena rasped in a voice several octaves lower.

Dennis sat up straighter at the tone of her voice and how the words seemed to roll over his body in waves, suddenly making him acutely aware of the beginnings of his own arousal.

"When you say things like that, I feel like you're deliberately trying to see me as a kid. But why? Is it so you can continue to lie to yourself about how you do not want me?"

Dennis, too stunned for words, felt his mouth drop open. But Elena merely chuckled.

"I could show you how much of a teenager I'm not."

"Elena..." Dennis heard himself whisper. The woman was putting him in his place without even trying. He had always had the upper hand when it came to women, so what was it about Elena that had him always blinking in surprise?

He had only met this woman hours earlier. How was she managing to reel him in so?

But Elena just sipped from her glass of water and said. "We cannot stare at each other like this all afternoon. We have to find something to occupy ourselves with."

Dennis could think of very interesting things that could keep them occupied for the remainder of the day. "Do you play board games?" he asked.

"You mean the one where the loser gets to lose an article of clothing every passing minute?"

Dennis blinked and then looked away. Was it just him, or was Elena making their conversation very sexual?

"We could do something else. Why don't you suggest something?"

"Conversation, perhaps? We've only met today, even though I've heard a lot about you and how well you do in the field."

"What's it going to be like? Twenty questions?" Dennis asked, already prickled with unease.

"Light talk to while the afternoon away. Or I can go sightseeing," she said, already beginning to get up.

"You can do no such thing."

"And you're the one to stop me? This entire debacle is stupid."

"Didn't you say you came here to ensure Adam's safety?"

"Yes. But not that way. Adam can very well take care of himself. We both know he's really going through it. It's the only plausible reason for leaving us in a bar to go fuck some woman."

"People do that all the time. It's not too untoward."

"Well, there's that. But there's no way I'm going to be cooped up here all evening—" but her stomach growled loudly, interrupting her little rant. Dennis tried not to laugh.

"I guess your stomach just about settles it," Dennis said, highly amused. They settled on pizza, and Dennis called to place the order. When he dropped the phone, he found Elena watching him.

"What?" he asked.

Elena simply shook her head. "I'm just trying to figure you out."

Dennis, suddenly curious about what she had just said, asked, "What do you mean?"

"I'm a woman, and I know when a man finds me attractive. I have seen the way your eyes have run over my body. I'm far from being oblivious to that. What I cannot, however, wrap my head around is how you have managed to think of me as someone awfully too young to be wanted."

"What?" Dennis croaked.

But Elena, without answering, stood up and moved towards him, her enchanting blue eyes never leaving his. She didn't walk so much as saunter, her narrow hips swinging from side to side. "This is what I mean," she whispered when she got close enough, her feminine scent drifting into his nostrils, causing his nose to flare.

Elena slinked her body against his so that her pert breasts brushed against his chest. Dennis swallowed hard, not quite believing what was happening.

But Elena simply stood on tiptoes and allowed her lips to brush against his stubbled jaw. Shockingly and suddenly aroused, Dennis found himself drawing the willowy woman against his body, crushing her soft curves against his much harder body and tilting her head back to claim those lips that had caught his attention the moment he'd set eyes on her.

Elena's lips were soft and pliant, kissing him back with desperation and heat. Her bottom lip was soft and damp, causing a little growl to crawl up his throat. Dennis could not quite believe that this was happening. Were they both high? Or simply drunk on the tension that had ricocheted between them?

Needing to have her, to get a better taste, Dennis nipped hard on Elena's lower lip and swung his tongue into the moist heat of her mouth as her lips parted in a gasp.

She tasted even better, the last traces of alcohol mixing with the natural taste of her that had him moving his hands to her beautiful, luxurious hair, marveling at its texture and suppleness. Dennis, eager to learn more of her, moved curious fingers to her shoulder blades and down her arms, feeling the goosebumps that awoke at his touch and the slight shiver that chased up and down her spine.

Dennis could not remember the last time he wanted a woman this much. The last time all he could think about was claiming a woman's body in the most primal way possible. But he wanted it with Elena, wanted to show her how much of a woman he thought she was, and how well he could play with her body and put that smart mouth to good use.

Panting, Dennis broke the kiss off, chuckling when Elena gave a little mewl of protest. He pressed hot lips against the soft smooth flesh of her neck, and he growled at how perfect Elena's skin tasted. But before he could explore her further, Elena dragged him back to her lips, and he sighed in pleasure as he gave in, kissing her back, matching her slow sensual pace.

When he slipped his fingers beneath her shirt, Elena gave a pleasurable moan, the sound reverberating through him, causing him to want her even more, want her naked and ready for him.

When Elena broke the kiss and stepped back, Dennis blinked, trying to clear the fog of lust.

"Your phone," she gasped out, her chest heaving up and down. Her eyes had darkened to a deep enchanting blue and her lips, oh her beautiful lips, were swollen and red and so tempting he had to physically take a step back, afraid he was going to do something very barbaric, like fuck her right then and there.

He moved to the coffee table and picked up his phone, a frown marring his features when he read the caller ID.

"Barton," he said the moment he brought the phone to his ear. The endorphins that had swept through him just seconds earlier were completely gone, and in their place was dread. Because Barton only ever called when something had gone awry or if there was a next assignment for them. There was no way Barton was calling to discuss the weather or what they'd had for breakfast.

"Dennis," came Barron's baritone voice. "Your partner is in danger." Barton, his superior, informed him without mincing words, going straight to the point.

"What?" Dennis choked, almost doubling over from shock.

"You know how I hate to repeat myself. I want you out of Las Vegas this instant. We cannot afford to have another one of us exposed."

"I'm afraid I cannot do that. There's someone under my care."

"What?"

"Mr. Fletcher's sibling is currently under my care."

"Then take her with you. Another untimely exposure is not something we can afford. I need you on the next assignment, Carnell. Take what you need from whomever, but your ass better not be busted."

"But what about Adam? Is he alright?" Dennis asked, eyes already closed in silent prayer. If Adam had gone and got himself killed, he was going to beat him to a pulp.

"He's alright. A rescue team has been sent to his location. He will be brought back to the facility, but you have to get yourself to safety."

"Alright," Dennis said, still in a state of disbelief.

"Another thing, what the hell were you all doing at a bar so late in the afternoon?"

Dennis winced. "Trying to be normal citizens and not the government's spies?"

Barton sounded very unimpressed when he said, "The next time I call you, I'd better hear that you're in a helicopter headed to a safe facility." And with that, he disconnected.

When Dennis turned to Elena, he found her eyes wide and already brimming with tears. Had she listened in on the whole conversation? "Is he alright?"

Dennis nodded. Elena turned away from him and said, "Where do we go now?"

"A facility. We have to keep you safe. If they've found your brother out, it won't be long before they seek out his weak points."

"Weak points?" Elena turned to him, fear and pain evident in her eyes.

"They know Adam will never give them what they want. So, they'll go after the weaker link. Something they know he doesn't want to lose or in your case, someone.

Elena covered her mouth with her hands, but Dennis was already striding to the bedroom to snap shut his little suitcase. "Come on," he said, taking Elena's hand in his and hurrying to his car.

Chapter Five

Elena was awfully quiet beside Dennis, whose mind had gone haywire. How had Adam been found? Dennis drove fast, his tinted windows rolled up. He knew at this point that taking a helicopter was going to draw attention to them like a neon sign.

Dennis allowed himself to think about everything that had happened in the past 12 hours except the one thing that had nearly an hour ago happened in his living room. What had he been thinking, taking Elena in his arms and kissing her like that?

He should have had better control of the situation, should not have been sucked into her eyes or played into her little game like he had. Now that she was in danger, he had to do everything to protect her, and that meant not trying to stir up anything between them. At this point, he hoped he had not completely ruined everything.

"Do you think Adam is safe?" Elena asked.

Dennis nodded. He needed to reassure her as much as himself. But their team was one of the best, and so he was nearly certain that the rescue team was going to get to Adam in time.

"He'd better be," she said as she leaned more into the car seat, her head turned to the window to watch the trees as they flew past.

Five minutes later, Elena was turning again to him. "Where are we going?"

"Somewhere safe."

“It has to have a name,” she snapped, which caused Dennis to turn to her. He didn't need to wonder about who had pissed in her Cheerios but understood how upsetting the sort of event that had just occurred was. They didn't know if Adam was truly safe and she, at that moment, could very well be in danger.

"It's a facility."

"I don't think I'll feel safe there."

"It's not about feeling it but actually being. You'd not come to harm there."

"I'd very much prefer to keep normalcy. I didn't come here for this. There's still time to return to California. I can still book tickets," Elena said, pain evident in her eyes.

Dennis ground his teeth hard to keep the harsh words on the roof of his mouth at bay. Was she being deliberately obtuse or did she not understand how very ugly this could turn out to be?

"Going back to California is off the table."

"You cannot force me to go to some stupid facility."

"Then we'd go somewhere else. Is that okay?" he said, shocked that he was actually giving in. He was supposed to stand his ground and ensure she followed through with his order, but the last thing he wanted was for her to feel like a puppet of some sort.

"Good," she said, turning away from him once more. Dennis, who could not stand the silence in the car, turned the radio on, allowing the voice of the broadcaster to drown out the silence.

"I didn't see this happening."

He had almost missed what she had said as she had turned away from him, still facing the window.

"What?" He questioned her, to hear her more clearly.

"I didn't expect this to be the outcome of my visit. I have a job to go back to."

Dennis, who was now curious, wondered about what she had wanted to say. Was there someone back home waiting for her return? Did she have someone in her life? If she did, why the hell had she come onto him like that?

Anger coursed through him at the thought that Elena had only played games with him.

"So, you have someone back home?" He asked, wondering why the thought of Elena with another man made him angry so.

"I didn't say that," she snapped, turning eyes that looked like they were spitting fire on him.

"What did you mean by what you said?"

"I don't have to have someone back home to, to want to go back to my life," she all but shouted. "And even if I did, it's none of your business."

"So, there's no one waiting for you back home?" he asked, wanting to know, needing clarification for his wildly beating heart to calm the fuck down.

"How's that your business?" she asked with a tight frown.

You made it my business by coming onto me like I was water in a desert. Something would have happened back at that apartment. We both know that.

Elena shook her head at him and simply turned away. Dennis did not understand why he was so angry when a fling was all he had always wanted from a woman. It wasn't like he wanted to push a ring down Elena's finger or anything, so why was he feeling so... jealous?

"I was simply trying to beat you at your own game. That kiss meant nothing."

Dennis frowned. That was supposed to be his line; he was supposed to say that, not her. "I hope you don't come back for a repeat," he ground out, anger causing the hand on his steering wheel to tremble.

Then Dennis drove for several hours, refusing to look away from the road. Even though he had just met Elena today, he couldn't help but feel like she was someone he knew and had always fought with. Whatever was going on between them was the oddest thing. He couldn't even wait for all this to be over.

"We won't make it to Arizona, so we spend the night here."

"We were going to Arizona?"

Dennis regarded her with cool eyes. "Of course, where did you think we were going? Heaven?"

Elena simply rolled her eyes and stepped out of the vehicle, and he did the same. When they got to the counter, there was a cute blonde with a pixie cut and several piercings so numerous it was ridiculous. The hotel wasn't five-star, but in that part of the city, it was one of the best they could find.

Her eyes trailed over Dennis appreciatively, something that did not go unnoticed by Elena, who scowled.

"One room?" she asked.

"Two please," Dennis corrected, pushing his credit card over at the same time Elena did hers, so that their fingers brushed in the process.

"Use mine," Elena all but sneered at the woman.

"Um," the woman started, confused and gazing at the two credit cards pushed her way.

"Can you both make a decision so I know whose credit card I should charge from?"

"Why do you think mine's on the counter?" Elena asked.

"Can you please put your damn card away?" Dennis glared hard at Elena, who glared right back.

"I can carry my own damn weight. I don't want you to take care of me as if I'm some child."

Dennis closed his eyes and counted to ten. He could just tell that this was going to be the most stressful week of his life. "How about I pay for this while you get dinner? We are supposed to be a team; come on."

Elena looked like she was thinking about it and finally nodded. "Alright," she said, finally taking her card off the counter.

"You are both cute," the blonde woman said as she swiped his card and handed it back alongside a key card.

"We will need two of those, one for my own room?"

"It's an ensuite, so there'll be no need for that."

"That's not what we asked for," Elena all but growled.

"But couples usually—"

"We are not a couple," Elena gritted out, her face slightly red. It would have been funny if Dennis wasn't feeling the same discomfort.

The blonde woman apologized and took back the key card, punching something into her system and handing over two key cards to them. As they moved towards the elevator, Dennis's phone rang out, and the display ID had his palm slightly sweating.

Adam. He gulped.

Elena paused and watched him with wide eyes.

"Denny."

"Are you alright? Are you back at the facility? Are you hurt? What did they do to you?" Dennis allowed the questions to flow past his lips.

"Nothing of the sort happened," Adam revealed. "The woman I went home with was one of them."

"One of them?"

"The gunmen we had apprehended a fortnight ago." Dennis could remember. The men, dangerous and sly, had managed to elude them at the last minute. But they had been able to save their target, Senator Brewer's little niece, which was all that had really happened.

"They know I worked with someone, but not who. They do not know you, Denny, which is why you are the only one who can truly keep Elena safe until they're apprehended."

Dennis nodded. "But she would still be safe at the facility."

Adam chuckled. "Did she even agree to go there? My younger sister is stubborn as a mule. There's no way anyone would be able to keep her cooped up in an underground facility."

"I've seen that," Dennis commented dryly.

"She's going to try to escape. Please keep her alive."

"She's refused to go to the facility. We will be in my Arizona townhouse tomorrow."

"Good, I trust you," Adam said. "I really have to go. Barton needs me to give a statement."

"Alright," Dennis agreed as the phone call was disconnected.

"Is he alright?" Elena asked, her eyes full of fear.

Dennis ignored the urge to wrap her in his arms and reassure her, and he said instead, "He's alright."

Elena nearly sank to the ground from relief. "Thank God."

"Come on," Dennis said as they headed towards the elevator. When they walked into the hallway, Dennis quickly sensed that something was wrong. There were men in suits casually coming upstairs. They looked absolutely normal except that they all had their hair scrapped, a signature look he knew was peculiar to only a particular set of gunmen.

"Elena," he began, "I am about to do something really reckless. Go with the flow so we can get out of here alive." That was all he said before pushing Elena against the wall and covering her lips with his in a passionate kiss, running his hands along her side profile to keep her face hidden.

He nipped hard on her lips, his heart soaring when she moaned. It sounded convincing, and her body suddenly arching into his didn't look like an act. Now, he was going to have to hope that the spies who were flooding the hallway would buy their act and not blow their heads off with the short pistol he had caught sight of.

9 798352 352083